With special thanks to Anne Marie Ryan
For my dear friend and fellow bookworm Maureen
Callahan-Wing, who let me be her bridesmaid

ORCHARD BOOKS

First published in Great Britain in 2018 by The Watts Publishing Group

1 3 5 7 9 10 8 6 4 2

Text copyright © Hothouse Fiction, 2018
Illustrations copyright © Orchard Books, 2018

The moral rights of the author and illustrator have been asserted.

A CIP catalogue record for this book
is available from the British Library.

ISBN 978 1 40835 113 0

Printed and bound in Great Britain by Clays Ltd, St Ives plc

The paper and board used in this book are made from wood from responsible sources.

Orchard Books
An imprint of
Hachette Children's Group
Part of The Watts Publishing Group Limited
Carmelite House
50 Victoria Embankment
London EC4Y 0DZ

An Hachette UK Company
www.hachette.co.uk
www.hachettechildrens.co.uk

Series created by Hothouse Fiction
www.hothousefiction.com

Bridesmaid
Surprise

ROSIE BANKS

Wishing Star Palace

The Secret Princess Promise

"I promise that I will be kind and brave,

Using my magic to help and save,

Granting wishes and doing my best,

To make people smile and bring happiness."

Story One

CHAPTER ONE
Weekend with Dad

"Can I have cheese on my burger, please?" asked Mia Thompson. Her mouth watered as a delicious smell wafted from the barbecue.

"One cheeseburger, coming right up," said Mia's dad, flipping a burger high up into the air with a grin.

"I want a sausage too!" called out Mia's little sister, Elsie.

Mia and Elsie were spending the weekend at their dad's flat. Most of the time they lived with their mum, but every other weekend they visited their dad. It had been hard to get used to at first, but now Mia and Elsie looked forward to their weekends with Dad – he always planned fun things to do with them.

"Come on, Elsie," said Mia. "Let's go and set the table."

The girls crossed the tiny garden and went into the kitchen through the patio doors. Opening a cupboard, Mia took out plates and drinking glasses while Elsie rummaged in the cutlery drawer for knives and forks.

Mia opened the fridge, which was covered in photos of the girls and pictures they'd drawn.

She took out a bowl of salad and a big bottle of lemonade.

"Ooh!" said Elsie excitedly. "Mum never buys fizzy drinks."

Mia and Elsie grinned at each other. There were definitely advantages to having two different homes!

"Don't forget the ketchup!" called Dad.

Mia and Elsie carried everything out to the garden and set the table on the patio.

"Perfect timing," said Dad, carrying over a 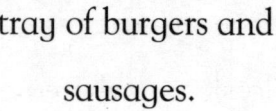 tray of burgers and sausages.

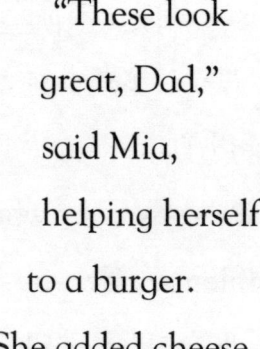

"These look great, Dad," said Mia, helping herself to a burger. She added cheese, lettuce, tomato and a big squirt of ketchup, then sandwiched it all in a bun.

"How's school, girls?" asked Dad, biting into his sausage.

"I got to take my class's pet hamster home last weekend," said Elsie proudly.

Dad chuckled. "I bet Flossie loved that."

Flossie was the girls' pet cat. "We didn't let Flossie anywhere near the hamster," Mia assured her father.

"And my class went on a day trip to the zoo," said Elsie.

"I remember when my class went to the zoo," said Mia. "It was really fun. Charlotte and I helped feed the lemurs."

"Are you still in touch with Charlotte?" asked Dad.

"Of course," said Mia. Charlotte was her best friend. She and her family had moved to America a while back.

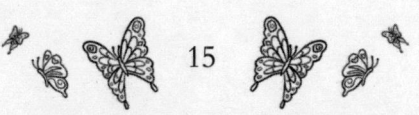

"Are her family enjoying the California sunshine?" asked Dad.

"They love it out there," Mia said.

"I bet you miss her," said Dad.

"We email and talk on the computer all the time," said Mia. What she couldn't tell her dad – or anyone else for that matter – was that she and Charlotte still got to see each other lots!

Shortly before Charlotte had moved, the girls had got the best surprise ever. They had been chosen to become Secret Princesses, who could grant people's wishes using magic! Mia and Charlotte were still doing their Secret Princesses training, but they met at Wishing Star Palace, an amazing palace in the clouds, and got to have magical adventures together.

When they'd finished eating, Dad patted his belly. "I'm stuffed. Shall we have a game of badminton to work off our dinner?"

"I'll play, Daddy!" cried Elsie, running over to get the racquets.

"What do you say, Mia?" Dad asked, ruffling her long, blonde hair.

"I can't," said Mia, sighing. "I've got lots of homework to do."

"Good, get it out of the way now,"

said Dad. "Then we can enjoy the weekend."

As Elsie and Dad batted shuttlecocks over the net that stretched across the lawn, Mia went indoors. She walked down the hallway to the bedroom she and Elsie shared at Dad's.

Mia's side of the room was tidy, with posters of animals on the walls. Her craft supplies were neatly stored in plastic tubs and the creations she'd made decorated her side of the room. Elsie's side of the room was crammed full of dolls and cuddly toys. Her bed was unmade, the hot pink duvet in a heap on the floor.

At first it had been weird sharing a bedroom, but Mia had got used to it now. It was actually good fun having sleepovers with her sister every other weekend!

Tossing a teddy bear back over to Elsie's side
of the room, Mia sat down at her desk. She slid
her homework book out of her school bag and
opened it up to a list of ten spelling words.

Hmm, she thought, looking at the first word
– *adventure*. She tapped her pencil on the desk
as she tried to think up a
sentence. She wrote:
*I can't wait to
have an amazing
adventure with
my best friend.*

Mia glanced
down at the
special necklace
she always wore.

Her heart gave a little skip of joy when she saw that the gold pendant shaped like half a heart was glowing. She didn't have to wait a minute longer – she was going on an adventure with Charlotte right now!

Holding the pendant, Mia said, "I wish I could see Charlotte." Golden light spilled out of the necklace and swirled around Mia. As the magic whisked her away, Mia didn't worry about her dad and Elsie missing her. No time would pass here while she was gone.

A moment later, she found herself in the grand entrance hall of Wishing Star Palace. Her clothes had magically transformed into her princess outfit – a gorgeous golden dress, a diamond tiara and sparkling ruby slippers.

"Hi!" cried a girl wearing a pretty pink princess dress, a tiara and ruby slippers just like Mia's. Her brown curls bobbed as she ran over to give Mia a hug.

"Hi, Charlotte," said Mia, squeezing her best friend tight.

"I'm so excited to be here," said Charlotte, clapping her hands. The moonstone bracelet around her wrist was identical to the one Mia was wearing.

"Hello, girls," said a beautiful princess with cool red streaks in her strawberry-blonde hair who was descending the marble staircase.

"Alice!" Mia and Charlotte exclaimed.

They ran to hug their old babysitter. It was
thanks to Alice that they were here, because
she had recognised their talent for friendship
and invited them to train as Secret Princesses.

"I have a new piece of jewellery," she said,
holding out her hand to show them a gold

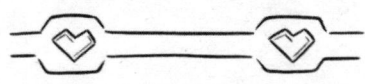

band with a huge,
sparkling diamond.

"Ooh, it's lovely,"
said Charlotte.

"Is it magic?" asked
Mia, peering at the
glittering diamond.

For completing the
third stage of their
training, the girls had

earned sapphire rings that flashed when danger was near.

"No, it isn't magic," replied Alice. "But it is very special." Her eyes twinkled merrily. "It's an engagement ring!"

CHAPTER TWO
The Wedding Bell

"Oh my gosh!" said Mia, her blue eyes widening in surprise. "That means—"

"You're getting married!" squealed Charlotte.

Alice beamed and nodded.

"Congratulations!" the girls cried.

Holding hands with Alice, they jumped up and down in excitement.

25

"Wait a sec," said Charlotte. "Who are you marrying?"

"His name is Matt," said Alice. "He's a musician in my band. We spent a lot of time together on tour – and we fell in love!"

Alice was a famous singer. She'd won a TV talent show and become a pop star, performing concerts around the world.

"I asked him to marry me when we were in Rome," Alice said, sighing dreamily. "It was so romantic."

"I'm really happy for you, Alice," said Mia.

"Thanks, sweetie," said Alice, giving her a kiss on the cheek.

"I can't wait to meet him," said Charlotte.

"I've told him all about you two," said Alice,

rumpling Charlotte's curls affectionately.

BUZZ! BUZZ!

Mia heard a soft buzzing noise. She suddenly realised that it was coming from her moonstone bracelet!

"Hello …" she said into the stone.

"Hi, Mia. It's Princess Cara," said a voice coming out of the stone. "Can you take Alice to the garden room, please?"

Charlotte gave Mia a curious look, but Alice hadn't even noticed Mia talking into her moonstone bracelet – she was too busy telling them about Matt.

"He's really funny and he's so talented," Alice gushed.

"Let's go to the garden room," Mia said.

They walked through the palace – past the elegant ballroom, the sunny drawing room and the formal dining room. The garden room was at the back of the palace, overlooking the beautiful grounds. It was filled with plants, presents – and princesses!

"Surprise!" shouted the Secret Princesses.

"Oh my gosh!" cried Alice, her hands flying to her mouth.

"We decided to throw you an engagement party," explained Princess Cara, who was wearing a trendy yellow dress. Her necklace had a pendant shaped like a thimble, because she was a talented fashion designer.

"I hope you're hungry," said Princess Sylvie, who had cherry-red hair and a cupcake

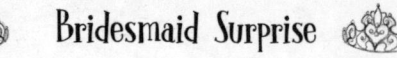

pendant on her necklace. In the real world she ran her own bakery. Sylvie waved her wand and scones, dainty sandwiches and tasty tarts magically appeared on the table.

"Weddings are so exciting!" said Princess Kiko, sitting down next to Alice. "I can't wait to hear what you're planning."

"We haven't planned anything yet," said Alice, laughing. "We only just got engaged!"

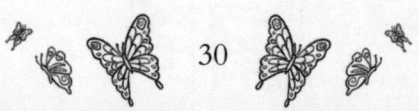

"I designed my own wedding dress," said Princess Cara. "It had a long lace train and pearl beading."

"It sounds beautiful," said Charlotte, spreading jam on a scone.

"I'm never getting married," said Princess Sylvie with a grin.

"Good! Everyone should do whatever makes them happy," said Alice, giving her a hug.

"I wore a white silk kimono and had one thousand and one origami cranes for decorations," Princess Kiko said.

"Ooh, that sounds beautiful! Why did you have so many?" asked Mia.

"For good luck," explained Kiko. "It's a Japanese tradition."

"Speaking of traditions," said Princess Anna, the oldest and wisest of the Secret Princesses, "we have our own wedding tradition here at Wishing Star Palace."

"The Wedding Bell!" exclaimed Princess Sylvie. "Let's go up to the Bell Tower now!"

Mia and Charlotte exchanged puzzled looks. Wishing Star Palace had four towers. One of them had a magic mirror. Another housed a magical telescope. But they'd never been to the Bell Tower before.

Everyone clicked the heels of their glittering ruby slippers together three times and called out, "The Bell Tower!"

A moment later, they were there. A huge gold bell hung down from the turret's roof.

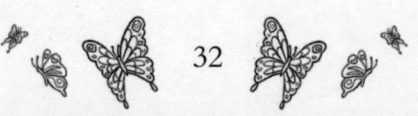

"Whenever a Secret Princess gets engaged," said Princess Anna, "we ring the Wedding Bell twice – once for the bride and once for the groom."

"What does that do?" asked Mia.

"The bell's magic brings happiness and good luck to their wedding day," explained Princess Anna, smiling.

The Secret Princesses took hold of the bell's long rope. But before they could ring it, there was a loud *CRACK*!

"What was that?" cried Charlotte.

"Oh no!" gasped Mia, looking up.

A jagged crack ran down the Wedding Bell. As they watched, black words formed on the bell's surface.

Someone's engaged, but Princess Poison's not glad,
 Love and happiness only make her mad.
The Wedding Bell's cracked and cannot ring,
Instead of good fortune, bad luck will it bring!

"I can't believe Princess Poison would do this," said Mia in dismay.

"Really?" asked Charlotte, raising one eyebrow.

Princess Poison had once been a Secret Princess, but she'd been banished from the palace for using her magic to gain power. Now she spoiled wishes instead of granting them, and caused trouble for the Secret Princesses with her cruel curses.

"How can we stop Princess Poison from spoiling Alice's wedding?" asked Mia.

"With love," said Princess Anna. "Love always triumphs over hate. We need to grant two special wedding wishes to break the curse."

The Secret Princesses all touched the bell with their wands. Two sad faces appeared on the bell – one on either side of the crack.

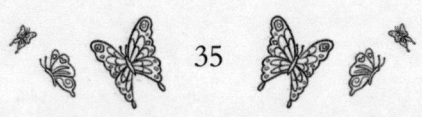

The girl on the left side was younger, with sandy shoulder-length hair. On the right side of the bell there was a dark-haired older girl, with cool flicks of black eyeliner and double-pierced ears.

"We need to grant their wishes," said Anna.

"Can we do it?" begged Charlotte. "Please?"

"Alice has done so much for us," Mia said. "It's our turn to help her."

"Thank you so much, girls," said Alice, smiling bravely.

"Touch the bell," said Princess Anna.

Mia and Charlotte placed their hands on the bell.

WHOOSH!

Magic lifted the girls away from the palace and set them down in a forest of tall pine trees. Their princess outfits had changed into leggings, T-shirts and trainers. Glancing up at the treetops, Mia noticed walkways of ropes and wooden planks. People wearing helmets and safety harnesses were slowly making their way across the walkways.

"Look!" said Charlotte. "There are the girls from the bell."

37

The two girls were standing by a sign that said *Welcome to Monkey Ropes*. The younger girl was looking anxiously at a lady. The older girl had her arms crossed over her chest and was standing next to a man with the

same dark hair and eyes as her.

"This will be a nice way for you girls to get to know each other better," said the lady.

The man nodded enthusiastically. "Violet loves this sort of thing."

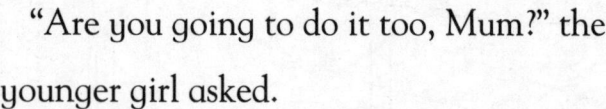

"Are you going to do it too, Mum?" the younger girl asked.

"No, Daisy," said her mum.

"But it says you need to be in groups of four," said Daisy, her voice trembling.

"We can be in a group with you!" said Charlotte, stepping forward.

The girl named Daisy smiled at them, revealing that she was missing a tooth.

"I'm Charlotte," said Charlotte. "And this is my friend Mia."

"I'm Daisy," said the younger girl. "And this is Violet. She's going to be my sister."

"STEPsister," the older girl corrected sharply.

Uh oh, thought Mia. *Violet doesn't sound happy at all!*

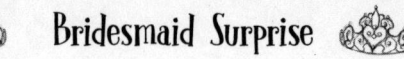

Mia and Charlotte exchanged a glance.
They had a lot of work to do – but luckily they
had magic to help them!

CHAPTER THREE
Things Get Ropey

As the four girls headed over to the starting point a phone rang. Violet pulled a mobile out of her jeans pocket.

"I'm at my dad's this weekend," she told the person on the other end. "He's forcing me to hang out with Daisy."

Mia and Charlotte looked at each other. Violet didn't sound very enthusiastic about

spending time with the younger girl.

"My mum is getting married to Violet's dad, Ben," explained Daisy. "Violet and I get to be bridesmaids."

"Cool," said Charlotte.

"So do you live together?" asked Mia.

"Not all the time," said Daisy. "Violet lives with her mum in a different town. But she's

going to visit most weekends."

"I've always wanted a big sister," said
Charlotte.

"Me too," said Daisy. "But I don't think
Violet likes me very much." She sighed. "I
really wish she did."

Aha! thought Mia, catching Charlotte's eye.
Now they knew Daisy's wish! They still had
to work out Violet's wish and make them both
come true – but it was a start!

"Come and get your safety briefing!" called
an instructor in a helmet, waving them over.

The instructor showed them how to adjust
their helmets and put on their harnesses.

Daisy's hands were shaking so much Mia
needed to help her tighten the straps.

"Thanks," said Daisy. "I'm kind of nervous."

"Me too," admitted Mia, looking up at the high ropes. When she wasn't granting wishes, she preferred to keep both feet on the ground!

"It's perfectly safe," said the instructor. She showed them how to use the clips on their harnesses. "Just remember, always stay clipped to the safety line."

The girls practised clipping and unclipping themselves to a thick metal wire.

"You two look like you've done this before," the instructor said to Violet and Charlotte.

"I did something similar on a school trip last year," said Violet, expertly unclipping herself. "It was awesome."

"My family loves rock climbing," said Charlotte, sounding excited.

"To get your certificates at the end," said the instructor, "your team needs to complete the course in an hour."

"Easy peasy!" said Violet, striding to the start of the course. She clipped herself to the safety line and quickly climbed up a rope ladder to a small wooden platform. Without looking back, she started making her way across a wobbly bridge suspended in the treetops.

"Do you want to go next?" Mia asked Daisy.

Daisy shook her head, looking terrified.

"What's wrong?" Charlotte asked.

"I'm scared of heights," Daisy admitted. "I only said I wanted to come because I wanted Violet to like me. What am I going to do?"

"Hurry up, slowcoaches!" shouted Violet from above.

"You heard what the instructor said," Mia told Daisy. "It's totally safe."

Daisy still looked reluctant.

"How about I go next?" said Charlotte. "Mia will go after you. That way we can both help you. Deal?"

Daisy nodded. Charlotte, who was good at anything sporty, nimbly scaled the ladder.

Taking a deep breath, Daisy bravely started to climb.

"You can do it!" Charlotte encouraged her from above.

"You're doing great!" cheered Mia from below.

Once Daisy had got to the top, Mia climbed up after her.

She stepped on to a wooden plank and made her way across the swaying bridge, gripping the safety line. Looking down, Mia gulped. She wasn't terrified of heights like Daisy, but it was a very long way down!

When they'd all made it across the wobbly bridge they reached a zip wire that stretched from the treetops down to the ground below.

"I love zip wires!" said Violet.

She clipped herself on and jumped off the platform.

"Whee!" she shrieked as she sailed to the ground, kicking up a cloud of dirt as she landed.

"I don't think I can do this," said Daisy, looking like she was going to be sick.

"Have you ever been on a zip line in a playground?" Charlotte asked.

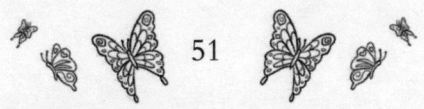

"Sure," said Daisy. "But it wasn't this high."

"Just close your eyes and imagine you're in the playground," suggested Mia.

"Come on!" cried Violet from the ground. "We've only got an hour!"

"I'd better go," said Charlotte. She jumped off and – *WHIZZ!* – zipped to the ground.

"Violet's going to think I'm such a wimp," said Daisy, trembling.

"She won't," said Mia. "Because you can do this. It will be fun – I promise."

Daisy squeezed her eyes shut. "Aaarrgghh!" she wailed as she whizzed down the zip line. When she reached the bottom, Violet helped Daisy unclip herself.

"Way to go!" Violet said, giving the younger girl a high five.

Daisy beamed with pride.

"Here I come!" shouted Mia. She jumped off the platform and sped down the zip line, laughing as her long hair blew in her face.

"That was actually amazing!" she cried when her heels hit the ground.

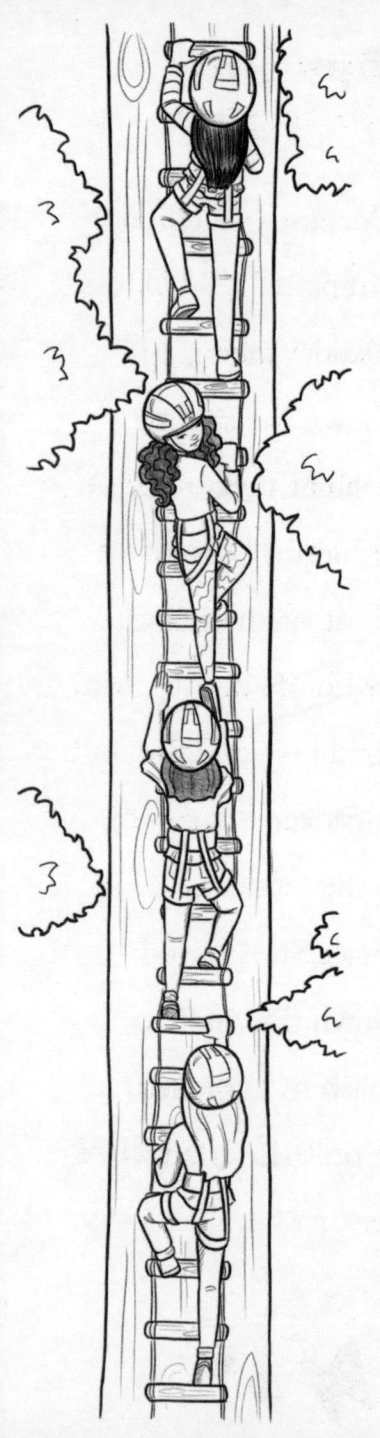

"Let's see what's next!" said Violet.

The next obstacle was a wobbly rope ladder made of logs. But at the top, the logs were spaced too far apart to reach.

Violet started climbing up the ladder.

"What are you waiting for?" she asked, looking over her shoulder.

"We need a plan," Mia said. "There's no way we can reach the top if we don't work together.

The logs are too far apart."

"Maybe we should work in pairs," said Daisy.

"Good thinking, Daisy," said Violet approvingly.

They all climbed up as high as they could on their own. Then, working together, Charlotte and Daisy gave Violet a boost up to the next level, and then they lifted Mia up. In turn, Mia and Violet reached down and pulled Daisy and Charlotte up behind them. Slowly but surely, they all reached the top of the ladder.

"Yes! We did it!" cried Violet.

She looked so happy that Mia decided to try and find out what her wish was. As they scrambled down a rope net on the other side of the ladder, Mia rushed over to Violet.

"Are you looking forward to the wedding, Violet?" she asked.

Violet shrugged, her smile fading. "I was happy with how things were before. I don't understand why it can't stay the same."

"It's hard when things change," Mia said sympathetically. "My mum and dad are divorced, too."

"I'm glad my dad's happy and Kate – Daisy's mum – is nice," said Violet. "But I don't need a new family. I've already got one."

"You'll always have that family. But now you'll have another family, too," said Mia. "Isn't two better than one?"

"I suppose so," said Violet, not sounding entirely convinced.

They moved on to
the last activity –
a climbing wall.
There were four
different paths up
the wall, each with
different coloured holds.

"What do you do?" asked Daisy.

"You work in pairs," said Charlotte. "The
person on the ground is attached to the climber
by a rope."

"It's brilliant," said Violet. "When you get to
the top you get to abseil down!"

"I don't think there's enough time left for us
all to climb," Mia said. "Charlotte and I can
stay on the ground."

Daisy looked up nervously. "I'm not sure."

"It will be a good way to get to know Violet," whispered Mia.

"OK," said Daisy bravely.

An instructor in a helmet came over, his head bent. "Use the red holds," he muttered, directing Daisy to the section of the climbing wall with red stones. He pointed Violet to the blue route.

Another instructor came over and checked their safety equipment. She showed Mia and Charlotte how to use a belay device. It allowed them to control the rope connecting them to their partners.

"The climbers won't fall even if they lose their grip," she explained.

Once she was sure Mia and Charlotte knew
what to do, the instructor told Violet and
Daisy, "You're good to go."

Violet shot off up the blue path, pulling
herself up the wall with the agility of a
mountain goat.

Daisy, however, was stuck. Halfway up the
wall, she stretched her arm out, desperately
trying to reach the nearest red hold.

"I can't do this," she said, sounding panicky.
"Violet's going to think I'm such a loser."

Mia suddenly noticed a blue light flashing. It
was coming from her sapphire ring!

"Charlotte!" she cried. "Danger's near!"

"That instructor!" Charlotte pointed at the
male instructor, who was smirking meanly as

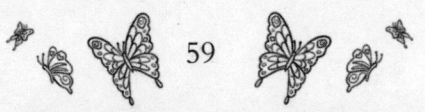

he watched Daisy struggle.

It was Hex – Princess Poison's horrible assistant!

CHAPTER FOUR
Room for Two

"What have you done?" Charlotte demanded.

"I sent Daisy up the most advanced path!" said Hex. "She'll never make it to the top." He walked off, chortling.

"Come on!" Violet called down from the top of the wall. "You're nearly there!"

Daisy clung on desperately to a red hold, unable to go any further.

"Daisy was really brave to try the rock climbing," said Charlotte. "We can't let Hex ruin this for her."

"Let's make a wish," said Mia.

The girls held their glowing half-heart pendants together.

"I wish for the red climbing path to be easier!" said Mia.

Light flashed out of the heart. Suddenly, the
red stones on Daisy's climbing wall weren't so
far apart any more.

"Try now," Mia called up to Daisy.

Daisy stretched out her arm and easily
grabbed the nearest red hold. She scrambled up
the rest of the wall.

"Way to go!" Violet said, when Daisy
reached the top.

"What do we do now?" Daisy asked.

"We abseil down," said Violet. "Just push
your legs off the wall and let yourself fall.
Ready?"

Daisy nodded nervously.

Mia and Charlotte let out their ropes.

"Woo hoo!" Violet and Daisy cried as they

abseiled down together.

When they reached the ground, Violet and Daisy unclipped themselves.

"That was really fun, Violet," said Daisy, her eyes shining.

"You can call me Vi," said the older girl as they took off their helmets and safety harnesses. "That's what my friends call me."

"OK … Vi," said Daisy, grinning.

"Well done, girls," said the real Monkey Ropes instructor. She presented them each with a certificate.

Violet and Daisy ran over to their parents, who were waiting by the entrance.

"How was it?" asked Daisy's mum.

"It was brilliant!" said Daisy.

Violet nodded. "Daisy was really brave."

"Vi helped me," said Daisy. "So did Mia and Charlotte. Can they come over for dinner? Pleeeeeease!"

"Is that OK with you, Vi?" Daisy's mum asked.

"Sure," said Violet. "That would be fun."

"Are your parents here?" Violet's dad asked.

"We need to check it's OK with them."

Mia and Charlotte exchanged anxious looks. What were they going to do?

An idea came to Mia in a flash – she could use her moonstone bracelet!

"Hang on a minute," she said. "I've got to make a call."

Stepping away from the others, she spoke into the white gem. "We need help!" she said, hoping that the Secret Princesses would get the message.

A moment later, Princess Anna appeared out of thin air. She was wearing jeans and a top rather than her princess gown.

"Thank you so much for coming!" said Mia, relieved to see her.

"No problem," said
Princess Anna, smiling.
"That's what your
moonstone bracelet is for."

"Hi," said Princess Anna,
going over to the grown-ups.
"I'm Anna. The girls are
with me."

"Daisy and Violet would
love for Mia and Charlotte
to come over for dinner,"
said Daisy's mum. "They all got on so well
together."

"That's absolutely fine," said Princess Anna.
She noted down the address and arranged to
pick the girls up after dinner.

67

"Have fun," said Anna, hugging Mia.

"Thanks," Mia whispered.

In the car, Daisy and Violet chatted for the whole drive home. Mia and Charlotte grinned at each other. At this rate, Daisy's wish would be granted in no time!

"Come on!" said Daisy. "I'll show you my – I mean, our – room!"

Mia and Charlotte followed Daisy and Violet upstairs.

The bedroom was painted pink and had twin beds with matching duvets. One bed was neatly made, with pretty cushions carefully arranged on it. The bedside table had a photo of Daisy and her mum, and a tidy stack of books. The other bed was unmade, with a

guitar case lying open on it. Piles of clothes, books and make-up were scattered all over the floor.

"I like your room," said Mia. It reminded her of the bedroom she shared with Elsie at her dad's flat.

"Thanks," said Daisy, pinning her Monkey Ropes certificate to a cork board above her bed.

"Would you mind if I took a quick shower?" Violet asked her guests, showing them her dirty hands. "I got really grubby today."

"That's fine," said Charlotte.

Scooping up some clothes, Violet headed to the bathroom.

"Want to play a game?" asked Daisy.

"OK," said Mia.

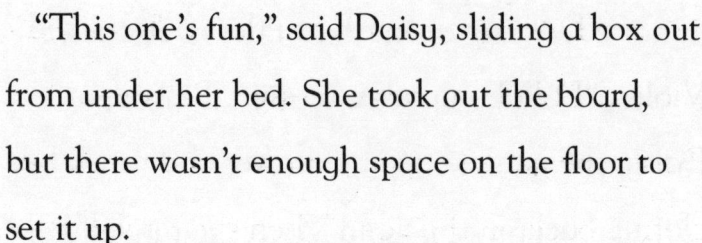

"This one's fun," said Daisy, sliding a box out from under her bed. She took out the board, but there wasn't enough space on the floor to set it up.

"I'll clear up a bit," she said.

She folded Violet's clothes and put them in the chest of drawers. Then she arranged Violet's make-up neatly on the dressing table. Gathering up the school books, Daisy packed them away in Violet's schoolbag.

"That's better!" said Daisy, setting up the game.

Just then, Violet came back, towelling her wet hair. Her eyes narrowed. "Where's all my stuff?" she demanded.

"I tidied it up," said Daisy.

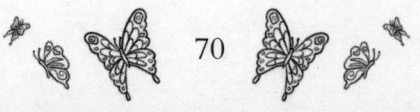

"How DARE you touch my things?" shouted Violet. "I LIKE my room messy." Glaring at Daisy, she yanked open a drawer and threw her clothes back on the floor. Then she tipped the contents of her schoolbag all over the floor.

"I'm so sorry," quailed Daisy. "I was just trying to be helpful."

"This is NEVER going to feel like home," yelled Violet. She stormed out of the room, slamming the door behind her.

"I didn't mean to upset her," said Daisy, her eyes brimming with tears. "I really want Violet to like me."

"It's hard getting used to sharing a room," said Mia sympathetically. "My sister and I share a room when we visit our dad. She's messier than me. We used to argue about it a lot, but it's OK now."

"How did you sort it out?" asked Daisy, sniffling.

"We each have our own half of the room," explained Mia. "And we leave each other's stuff alone."

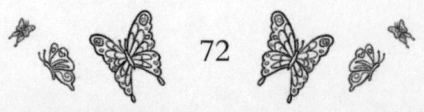

"I'll do that too," said Daisy. "I want Vi to like coming here."

"Why?" demanded a harsh voice. "This used to be YOUR room. Why should you have to share?"

Mia spun around and saw a tall woman in a green dress. She had jet-black hair with a blonde streak, and cold green eyes.

Daisy gasped. "Who are you?"

"I'm Princess Poison," said the woman. "And

today's your lucky day! I'm here to grant your
wish of getting your room back."

She pointed her wand at Violet's side of the
room and said a spell:

Get rid of Violet's messy stuff.
Show her that enough's enough!

Green light shot out of the wand and all of
Violet's belongings vanished.

"What have you done?" Daisy cried. "I didn't
want to get rid of Violet's stuff – I just wish
that she liked me!"

"Oops!" said Princess Poison. "I guess I
misunderstood." She gave a wicked smile then
waved her wand and disappeared in a bright

flash of sickly green light.

Daisy sank down on Violet's bed – the only thing left on that side of the room.

"Violet will think I did this," Daisy wailed. "She'll never like me now." Burying her face in her hands, she started sobbing.

"Please don't cry, Daisy," said Charlotte. "Mia and I can help you."

Daisy looked up, her eyes red and swollen. "Really?"

Mia nodded. It was time to use another wish!

CHAPTER FIVE
Cooking up Trouble

Mia and Charlotte held their pendants together.

"I wish for Daisy and Violet's bedroom to be perfect for both of them," said Charlotte.

POOF! The bedroom was magically transformed. Huge tissue-paper flowers hung down from the ceiling and strands of flower-shaped fairy lights stretched across the room.

Daisy's side of the room was still pale pink and neat as a pin, but now a pretty folding screen divided the room in two. The other half of the room was painted vibrant purple. Violet's guitar case was propped against an unmade bed, her dressing table was cluttered with lotions and potions, mounds of clothes were scattered on the floor and her desk was covered in books – just the way she liked it.

"What's going on?" asked Daisy, rubbing her eyes. "First that lady turned up and made all of Violet's stuff vanish. Then you two got everything back – AND changed the room. Am I having some sort of weird dream?"

"It's not a dream," said Mia.

"It's magic," said Charlotte.

Daisy scratched her head. "How is that even possible?"

"Mia and I are training to become Secret Princesses," explained Charlotte. "We're here to grant your wish."

"Was that lady a princess too?" asked Daisy.

"Princess Poison used to be a Secret Princess but she isn't one any more. She was only pretending that she wanted to grant your wish," said Mia. "Really she wants to spoil it."

"We won't let her, though," Charlotte added quickly.

"Do you like how your room looks?" asked Mia.

"I love it," said Daisy. "But what on earth will Violet say?"

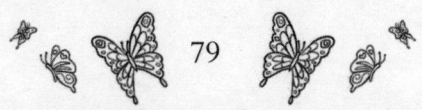

"She won't realise that anything's changed; it's part of the magic," Charlotte explained. "Wait and see!"

They didn't have to wait long. Violet came back to the room, her hair in French plaits. She flopped down on the bed, no longer cross and not seeming to notice anything strange.

"I like your hair, Vi," Daisy said.

"Thanks," said Violet. "Want me to do yours for you?"

"Yes, please!" said Daisy.

Violet patted her bed. "Come and sit down over here."

As she plaited Daisy's hair, Violet said, "Maybe sharing a room won't be so bad."

Daisy grinned in delight.

"I'm glad Violet's happier," Mia whispered.

"But what do you suppose her wish is?"
Charlotte murmured.

Mia had nearly forgotten about Violet's
wish. They really needed to find out what it
was, or they wouldn't be able to break Princess
Poison's curse!

A rumbling noise interrupted Mia's thoughts.
"What was that?" she asked.

"It was my tummy," said Daisy, rubbing her belly. "I'm starving."

"Me too," said Violet. "I wonder if Dad's started cooking dinner yet."

"They're probably busy with wedding plans," said Daisy. "They've got so much to do."

Mia thought about all the times she'd cooked with Elsie. It was one of her favourite things to do with her sister.

"Hey!" said Mia. "Maybe you two could cook dinner as a surprise."

"That's a great idea!" said Violet.

"But I don't know how to cook," said Daisy.

"Don't worry," said Violet. "I'll show you what to do."

"We'll help too," offered Charlotte.

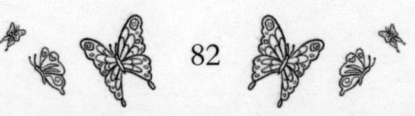

The girls headed to the kitchen. Daisy pulled some cookbooks off a bookshelf. "What should we make?" she asked Violet.

"This looks yummy," said Violet, pointing to a recipe for a creamy pasta dish.

"It does look good," said Daisy. "But we had pasta last night."

"I'm not fussy," said Violet. "The only thing I hate is mushrooms." She shuddered. "They're so slimy."

"I hate Brussels sprouts," said Daisy, pulling a face. "And walnuts."

Flipping through a cookbook, Violet stopped at a recipe for curry. "Do you like spicy things?"

"Ooh, yes!" said Daisy. "Mum and I both really like Thai food."

"So do Dad and I," said Violet. "Let's make a red curry." Checking the list of ingredients, she said, "And best of all, it doesn't have mushrooms, Brussels sprouts or walnuts!"

Opening the cupboard, Violet took out rice, and a jar of red curry sauce. Daisy found chicken and vegetables in the fridge.

As Violet cut the chicken into small chunks,

Charlotte chopped up an onion.

"Hey," said Charlotte. "What's round and white and giggles?"

"I don't know," said Daisy. "What?"

"A tickled onion," said Charlotte, waggling her eyebrows.

Chucking, Violet swatted her gently with a tea towel. "That's a rubbish joke."

Mia looked at Violet thoughtfully. She seemedmuch happier – but they still didn't know what her wish was!

"Let's have some music," said Daisy, turning on the radio.

A beautiful voice was belting out a pop song.

"Oh, I love Alice de Silver," said Violet, starting to sing along.

"You have a really nice voice," said Daisy.

"Thanks," said Violet. "I play the guitar in a band with some kids at school. Do you play any instruments?"

"I take piano lessons," said Daisy.

"Cool," said Violet. "You'll have to play me something."

Soon the red curry was bubbling on the hob. Mia and Charlotte helped the girls tidy up.

"Do you mind keeping an eye on the curry?" asked Violet. "I want to call my mum."

"No worries," said Daisy, stirring the curry as Violet went upstairs.

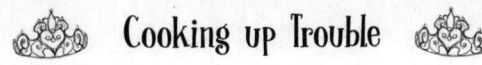
"Mmm," said Mia, inhaling the scent of garlic, coconut and lemongrass. "It smells really delicious."

"Oh dear. I think you forgot something," said Princess Poison. She had magically appeared out of nowhere.

"Not you again," groaned Charlotte.

"I'm afraid so," said Princess Poison. She lifted the cooking pot's lid and peered inside. "I think you've left out an important ingredient."

Pointing her wand at the pan, Princess Poison gave a nasty smile and said:

Mushrooms are what you forgot to add.
I'll put in loads and make it taste bad!

Bad magic flashed out of the wand. Huge, slimy mushrooms bobbed about in the simmering curry.

"But Violet hates mushrooms!" Daisy cried out in dismay.

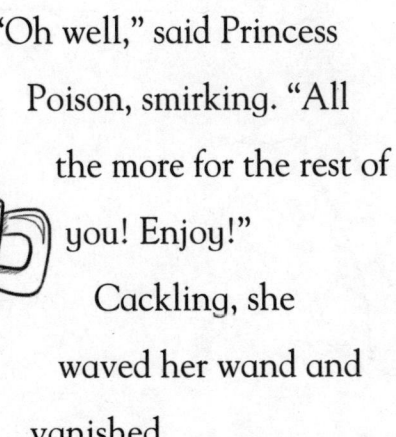

"Oh well," said Princess Poison, smirking. "All the more for the rest of you! Enjoy!"

Cackling, she waved her wand and vanished.

Daisy burst into tears. Charlotte and Mia rushed to hug her.

"What are we going to do?" Daisy sobbed. "Dinner's completely ruined!"

CHAPTER SIX
Curry in a Hurry

"Violet's going to think I added the mushrooms on purpose," said Daisy. "She'll hate me!"

Mia looked down at her necklace. The half-heart pendant was glowing very faintly now. There was only a little magic left. "Let's use our last wish," she said.

Charlotte pressed her pendant against Mia's. "I wish for a delicious dinner!" she said.

Golden light spilled from the necklace. Suddenly, the dining table overflowed with a Thai feast – with no mushrooms in sight. There were bowls of curry, coconut rice, fried noodles, crispy spring rolls and satay skewers.

"Thanks for setting the table, Daisy," Violet said, returning to the kitchen. "This looks great."

Violet's dad wandered in, sniffing the air. "Something smells good in here."

"Oh my!" said Daisy's mum, noticing the full table.

"Surprise!" said the girls.

"It was so thoughtful of you to make dinner," said Daisy's mum.

"Yes, thank you," said Violet's dad, popping

a spring roll in his mouth.

They all sat down and helped themselves to the spicy food.

"Yum!" said Daisy, dipping a chicken skewer in peanut sauce.

"How are the wedding plans coming along?" asked Violet.

"We've finally set a date," replied her dad, taking another helping of curry. "We're getting married on the tenth of June."

"It's going to be on my friend Kim's farm," said Daisy's mum. "We want it to be fun and informal – a big party for all our friends and family."

Listening to Kate and Ben discuss their wedding made Mia think about Alice. She deserved to have a wonderful wedding, too. For that to happen, they really needed to grant Daisy's wish – and Violet's, too.

After dinner, Kate said, "That was delicious, thank you. We're going to take a walk to get some fresh air." Linking arms, she and Violet's dad headed out into the evening.

"They're so cute together," said Mia.

The girls wandered into the living room. Daisy sat down at the piano and played a few notes.

"Have you got them a wedding present yet?" Violet asked Daisy.

Daisy shook her head. "I want to get something special, but I haven't thought of anything yet."

"Same here," said Violet.

"Why don't you make something?" Mia suggested.

"But what?" asked Violet.

Daisy plinked and plonked a few more keys on the piano as they all tried to think of the perfect idea.

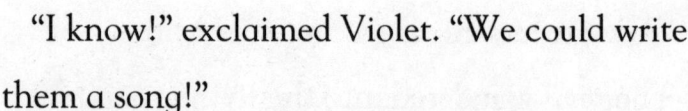

"I know!" exclaimed Violet. "We could write them a song!"

"Yes!" cried Daisy. "They'd love that!"

Daisy and Violet sat together on the piano bench. As Daisy picked out a melody on the piano, Violet scribbled down lyrics.

"You're getting married today, hooray!" Violet sang. "We wish you joy on your wedding day!"

Mia whispered, "They're getting along!"

"Let's hope Princess Poison doesn't turn up again and wreck things," murmured Charlotte.

"OK, I think we've got it," said Violet. "I'm going to get my guitar so I can play along." She ran upstairs.

"Can I join in with your little sing-along?"

cooed Princess Poison,
appearing once more.

"No!" said
Charlotte.

Princess Poison
pointed her wand at
the song the girls had just
written. "Violet will be singing a different tune
when she thinks you ruined the song."

"No!" cried Daisy, clutching the piece of
paper to her chest. "Please don't do that!"

"Who are you?" demanded Violet, coming
back with her guitar. "What's going on?

"She's going to destroy our song!" said Daisy.

Violet stood in front of Daisy, bravely
shielding her from Princess Poison.

"Get out of here!" Violet shouted. "Leave my little sister alone!"

Daisy threw her arms around Violet, who hugged her back.

The piano magically started to play the tune the girls had just written!

Mia and Charlotte grinned at each other. They knew that the

music was because Daisy's wish had been
granted – and so did Princess Poison!

"Don't look so pleased with yourselves,"
growled Princess Poison. "Your friends at the
palace won't be ringing the Wedding Bell any
time soon. It takes more than one wish to break
my curse!" Slashing her wand through the air,
she disappeared.

Mia, Charlotte and Daisy all breathed a sigh
of relief.

"Um, can someone please tell me what that
was all about?" said Violet.

"It was magic!" Daisy blurted out. "That
mean lady is a bad princess but Mia and
Charlotte are good princesses. They granted
my wish that you would like me!"

"Slow down!" said Violet "You wished that I would like you?"

Daisy nodded sheepishly.

"I do like you," said Violet. "I always have. I'm just finding it a little hard to get used to having two families – and a new little sister. But today has helped me to see that it's going to be fine."

She turned to Mia and Charlotte. "You two are magic princesses?" she asked.

"Well, we're not princesses yet," said Mia.

"But we can do magic," added Charlotte.

"We granted Daisy's wish and we want to grant yours, too," said Mia.

"The only problem is we don't know what it is," said Charlotte.

"That's easy," said
Violet, laughing.
"I wish for Dad
and Kate to
have a perfect
wedding day!"

*DING
DONG!*

The girls answered the door. It was Princess
Cara and Princess Anna.

"Time to go home, girls," said Princess Anna.

"Goodbye," said Daisy, hugging Mia and
Charlotte. "Thanks for everything."

"We'll see you on the wedding day," said
Charlotte.

"To grant Violet's wish," added Mia.

"Great work, girls," said Cara once they were outside.

"We can come back to grant Violet's wish, right?" asked Charlotte.

"So we can make sure that Alice has a happy wedding," said Mia.

"Of course," said Anna. "But now you need to go home."

She waved her wand and a moment later Mia was back at her dad's house. Looking down at her homework, she saw that her next spelling word was *excited*.

A sentence popped into her head straight away. Picking up her pencil, she wrote:

I'm really excited because I'm going to a wedding soon!

Story Two

CHAPTER ONE

An Exciting Invitation

"Be patient, greedy guts," said Mia, laughing as Flossie purred and rubbed against her legs. Crouching down, Mia shook dry food into the cat's bowl.

"Hey, Mia!" said Elsie, holding a piece of jigsaw puzzle. "I need your help!"

"OK," said Mia, following her little sister out into the hallway.

PLOP!

Catalogues and envelopes dropped through the letterbox and landed on the floor.

"Mum!" Mia cried, gathering them up. "The post has come."

Mum came downstairs, holding a laundry basket. She put the laundry down and took the post from Mia.

"This looks posh!" said Mum, opening a thick, cream-coloured envelope. She pulled out a fancy invitation with swirly gold writing.

"Alice is getting married!" Mum exclaimed. "And she's invited us all to the wedding!"

"Yay!" cheered Elsie. "We're going to a wedding!" She grabbed a towel from the laundry basket and draped it over her

head. "Dum dum dee dum," Elsie hummed, pretending to be a bride.

"What a lovely surprise!" Mum said.

Mia did her best to act surprised. She was relieved that Alice had finally shared her happy news. It had been hard keeping it secret from her family!

Mum went over to the calendar and marked Alice's wedding day on it.

"How exciting!" Mum said. "I wonder if any other pop stars will be there."

Mia bit her lip anxiously. She was excited about Alice's wedding, too. But there was another wedding to go to first – Violet's dad was marrying Daisy's mum today! Mia had been counting the days until the tenth of June. Now that it had arrived, she couldn't stop checking her necklace to see if it was glowing yet. She and Charlotte had to grant Violet's wish to break Princess Poison's curse on the Wedding Bell. If they didn't, Alice's wedding wouldn't be blessed with happiness and good luck.

"Can we make Alice a wedding card?" Elsie asked, her jigsaw forgotten.

"Of course," said Mia. "I'll go and get my marker pens."

She hurried to her
bedroom and shut the
door behind her. Pulling
her necklace out of her
T-shirt, she saw that it
was glowing!

Holding the pendant,
she said, "I wish I could
see Charlotte." The light
streaming out of the necklace grew brighter
and brighter, wrapping Mia in its warm glow.
Mia grinned as the magic swept her away. She
and Charlotte were going to help Violet – and
Alice, too!

She landed in the entrance hall of Wishing
Star Palace, wearing her gold princess dress,

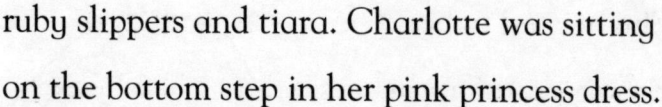

ruby slippers and tiara. Charlotte was sitting on the bottom step in her pink princess dress.

"Charlotte!" Mia cried, running over to hug her friend. "Did you get invited to Alice's wedding?"

"Yes," said Charlotte. "But I'm not sure if my family can go. Flights from California to England are really expensive."

"Oh, I hope you can come!" said Mia.

"Me too," said Charlotte. "But at least I get to see Alice at the palace." Standing up, she asked, "Where are the princesses, anyway?"

Mia heard the sound of excited chatter coming from down the hall. "I think they're in the kitchen," she said.

The big, sunny kitchen had gleaming copper

pots and pans hanging from the walls and gingham curtains at the windows. The Secret Princesses were gathered around a long wooden table, drinking tea and chatting animatedly.

"Hello, girls," said Alice, getting up to kiss Mia and Charlotte.

"We're helping Alice plan her wedding," explained Princess Ella, stroking a ginger kitten on her lap. "She hasn't even chosen her wedding cake yet!"

Wearing a polka-dotted apron over her princess dress, Princess Sylvie said, "Luckily she has us to help her. How about something like this ..." She waved her wand and a three-tiered wedding cake covered in pink and red icing flowers appeared on the table.

"Oooh!" exclaimed the princesses.

"Or maybe this," said Sylvie, flicking her wand again.

The wedding cake changed into a pyramid of golden cupcakes, frosted with edible glitter and sparkling silver balls.

"Yum!" said the princesses.

"I just can't decide!" said Alice.

Sylvie stroked her chin thoughtfully. "I've got it!" she said. She waved her wand and the cupcakes became a white chocolate layer cake, with dark chocolate musical notes decorating the sides. Best of all, there were tiny marzipan figures of Alice and Matt on the top layer.

"Oh, that's perfect!" said Alice.

"Let's see how it tastes," said Sylvie.

As everyone sampled slices of the rich chocolate cake, Princess Ella asked, "So have you picked out a wedding dress yet?"

Alice shook her head. "I've been so busy working on my next album I haven't even had time to go shopping."

"Who needs to go shopping when you've got a magic fashion designer?" said Princess Cara. She waved her wand and Alice's outfit changed into a wedding dress. It had puffed sleeves and a billowing skirt with layers and layers of tulle.

"Give us a twirl!" cried Princess Sylvie.

Alice modelled the dress for her friends.

"Nope, that's not right," said Cara, frowning. "You look like a meringue."

She waved her wand and the poufy wedding dress turned into a sleek, ivory-coloured sheath with sheer sleeves and pearl buttons down the back.

"Ooh, that's elegant," said Princess Ella.

"Yes," agreed Cara. "But I'm not sure it's quite right."

Another wave of the wand changed the ivory gown into a white leather mini dress.

"No way," said Alice.

"OK," said Cara. "I think I've got it."

With a final wave of Cara's wand, Alice was in a gorgeous gown. The strapless bodice flared out into a long skirt sparkling with crystal beads. A lace veil cascaded down Alice's back.

"It's gorgeous!" said Alice, beaming.

"You look so beautiful," said Mia.

"You look like the perfect bride," said Charlotte. "And we're going to make sure you have the perfect wedding day."

Suddenly, the Secret Princesses' wands began to flash.

"We've got to go and grant Violet's wish!" Charlotte cried.

"We won't let you down," Mia promised.

"I know you won't," said Alice, blowing them both kisses.

Clicking the heels of their ruby slippers together three times, Mia and Charlotte cried, "The Bell Tower!"

"Ready?" Mia asked Charlotte when they landed in the Bell Tower.

Charlotte nodded and they both touched the bell, which still had a jagged crack running down it. Mia's fingers tingled as the bell's magic pulled them away from the palace.

They were off to a wedding!

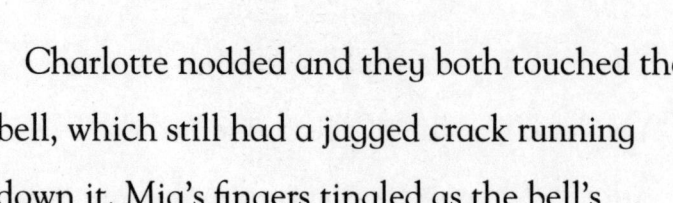

CHAPTER TWO

A Beautiful Barn

The magic set the girls down in the middle
of a farm. There was an old stone barn in the
distance. Nearby, there were horses grazing
in a field speckled with brightly coloured
wildflowers.

"Nice dress," said Mia, admiring Charlotte's
lacy, lemon-yellow frock. Her own outfit had
changed into a baby blue prom-style dress.

"I like yours too," said Charlotte. "It matches your eyes. But I can't figure out what we're doing in the middle of a field – I thought we were going to a wedding!"

"Don't you remember?" Mia reminded her friend. "Daisy's mum said they were getting married on her friend's farm."

"That's right!" exclaimed Charlotte.

"Those horses are gorgeous," said Mia, leaning against the fence. "I wish we could go and stroke them!"

"Not now," said Charlotte, tugging Mia gently. "We've got a wish to grant!"

The girls followed the path to the barn. Inside, they found Daisy and Violet blowing up balloons.

"Look, Vi!" cried Daisy. "Mia and Charlotte are here!"

"Wow!" said Violet, grinning as she tied a knot in a balloon. "You actually came. I was

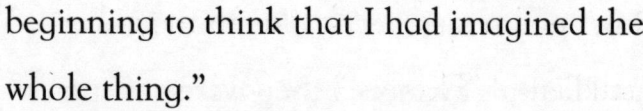

beginning to think that I had imagined the whole thing."

"I told you they'd come back," said Daisy, with a grin.

"We've got to grant your wish of the wedding being perfect," said Mia, smiling.

"What can we do to help?" asked Charlotte.

"You can help us decorate the barn," said Violet, handing them strings of bunting.

Climbing up on hay bales, Mia and Charlotte helped Daisy and Violet hang decorations around the old barn. Soon, the ancient wooden beams were covered with pretty floral-printed bunting and white balloons.

"What should we do next?" asked Mia.

Violet pulled a list out of her back pocket and studied it. "Flowers," she said.

They all went out into the meadow and picked bunches of wildflowers. As they filled baskets with red poppies, blue cornflowers and white daisies, Violet and Daisy chatted about the wedding.

"I just can't wait to be a bridesmaid," said Daisy.

"I know," said Violet. "My friends said I have to take loads of pictures."

"Daisy and Violet are still getting along well," Mia whispered as she picked a scarlet poppy.

"They seem really excited about the wedding," said Charlotte.

"We've got to make sure that nothing spoils it," said Mia.

"Don't you mean nobody?" said Charlotte.

They carried the baskets of wildflowers back to the barn. After arranging them into small bouquets, they put them in glass milk bottles filled with water.

"What did the bride say when she dropped her bouquet?" asked Charlotte. Waving a daisy in the air, she didn't wait for anyone to answer. "Whoops a daisy!"

Mia groaned at Charlotte's cheesy joke. She plucked the daisy out of her friend's hand and added it to a bouquet.

The girls put the milk bottle bouquets on trestle tables draped with white tablecloths. The tables were set with old-fashioned china and mason jars instead of wine glasses.

"Mum loves vintage stuff," explained Daisy.

Violet checked her list again. "We've got to put out the wedding favours."

"Look what we made," said Daisy, holding up a little bag filled with heart-shaped biscuits and tied with ribbon.

"That's adorable!" said Mia.

"They taste really yummy too," said Daisy. "Vi taught me how to bake them."

"We need to put one by every place setting," said Violet.

The girls scurried around the barn, leaving a party favour beside every plate.

"Phew!" said Violet, gazing around the barn. "I think we're done in here."

"It looks amazing," said Charlotte.

"Just in time, someone's coming!" said Daisy.

A tall, thin figure in an enormous green hat was tottering up the dirt path towards the barn. She was holding a huge gift-wrapped box.

"The wedding doesn't start for a few hours," said Violet, puzzled. "One of the guests must have got the time wrong."

"That's no guest," said Mia grimly.

"You're not invited," Charlotte told Princess Poison as she sauntered into the barn.

"When has that ever stopped me?" taunted Princess Poison.

"Don't worry, I won't stay long. I just wanted to drop off a little wedding present." She lifted the lid off the box and tipped out the contents.

PLOP!

A pile of manure landed on one of the beautifully set tables.

"What are you doing?" shrieked Violet. "That's disgusting!"

"But this is a barn," said Princess Poison. "I thought I'd help you make it more authentic."

She strode over to the door and pointed her wand at the horses in the field. Her eyes glittering with malice, she rasped out a spell:

There's a wedding in a barn, everyone's excited.
So let's make sure all the horses are invited.

Green light shot out of her wand and suddenly the horses from the field were inside the barn!

NEIGH! NEIGH!

The barn had been transformed into a dirty, smelly stable. The beautiful decorations had vanished and in their place were stinky piles of manure and buckets of feed. Flies buzzed around everywhere, bothering the horses.

"Now it looks like a proper barn," said Princess Poison.

"She's trying to ruin the wedding!" cried Daisy.

131

"Not just one wedding," said Princess
Poison. "Two weddings!" Turning to Mia and
Charlotte, she hissed, "Your princess pal's
wedding is going to be a disaster, too!"

Howling with laughter, Princess Poison
waved her wand and vanished in a burst of
green light!

CHAPTER THREE
A Dog's Dinner

"Don't cry, Daisy," said Violet, wrapping her arms around the younger girl.

"But Princess Poison is going to wreck the wedding," sobbed Daisy.

"No, she won't," Violet comforted Daisy. "Mia and Charlotte can help us fix this. Can't you?" she added hopefully.

"We'll try," said Charlotte.

"Let's get the horses out first," said Mia. She took a beautiful chestnut mare by the bridle and led it out of the barn.

"What did Princess Poison mean about spoiling two weddings?" asked Violet, taking a white horse with a black mane into the field.

"One of our princess friends is getting married, too," explained Mia.

"But don't worry," Charlotte assured the girls. "We won't let her spoil anyone's wedding."

Once all of the horses were grazing in the field again, the girls looked around the filthy barn. It smelled so bad that Mia had to hold her nose. There was only one way to get it cleaned up in time for the wedding.

"Let's use a wish," said Charlotte.

Pressing her half-heart pendant against Charlotte's, Mia said, "I wish for the barn to look beautiful for the wedding."

Magical light spilled out of the heart, transforming the barn. Twinkling white fairy lights were wrapped around the wooden beams and swathes of white silk were draped over them. Enormous bouquets decorated the tables,

and the girls' party favours were by every plate.
Hay bales topped with white cushions were
arranged in front of an archway of white roses.

Violet's dad stepped into the barn. "Wow!"
he gaped, grinning as he looked all around.

"This looks wonderful."

"Mia and Charlotte helped a lot," said Violet, smiling gratefully at the girls.

"Nice to see you again, girls," Ben said. "So glad you could come to the wedding."

"Where's Mum?" asked Daisy.

"She's getting ready in the farmhouse," said Ben. "I haven't seen her today. It's bad luck for the groom to see his bride before the wedding."

"It's also bad luck to see Princess Poison before the wedding," Charlotte whispered in Mia's ear.

"How's your speech coming along?" Violet asked her dad.

"I'm really nervous about it," said Ben. "Would you girls mind if I practised it?"

"Go for it, Dad!" said Violet.

The girls perched on hay bales and listened to Ben's speech. He explained how he had met Daisy's mum at a jumble sale, when they were both trying to buy the same antique radio.

"I let Kate have the radio," he said. "Then I bought her a cup of tea. We haven't stopped talking ever since." Then Ben told the story of how he had proposed at a fancy restaurant and got so nervous that he dropped the ring into Kate's soup!

"Aw!" said Mia. She loved romantic stories!

Smiling at Daisy and Violet, Ben said, "As if finding a wonderful woman to be my wife didn't make me the luckiest man alive, our marriage comes with an added bonus. Now, instead of having one amazing daughter, I'll have two!"

Daisy and Violet beamed at each other as Mia and Charlotte clapped loudly.

"That was brilliant, Dad," said Violet.

"I meant every word of it," said Ben, opening his arms wide to give both Violet and Daisy a big hug.

The sound of wheels crunching along the path came from outside the barn.

"That must be the caterers," said Ben.

They went outside. A white van with the words *Posh Nosh* written on its side parked behind the barn. People piled out and quickly set up a tent. Then they started unloading silver buffet dishes.

"Mmm," said Mia, as delicious smells drifted over to them.

"Hi, I'm Sandy," said a lady wearing a chef's hat and a white jacket. "Would you like to sample the food before the wedding?"

"I'm too nervous to eat a bite," said Ben. "But you girls go ahead. I'm going to go and freshen up."

"Yum," said Mia, tasting a spicy fishcake.

"Scrummy!" said Charlotte, tucking into a miniature cheeseburger.

"Does this have mushrooms in it?" asked Violet, holding up a tart.

"No," said the chef. "The bride requested a mushroom-free menu."

Violet bit into the tart. "Dee-lish!"

"Where's the wedding cake?" asked Daisy.

"Still in the van," said Sandy. "Thanks for reminding me."

She went over to the van and returned carrying a spectacular wedding cake. Pink and yellow icing roses tumbled down its three layers.

"Oooh!" the girls gasped.

"Want us to take it into the barn?" asked Violet.

"Thanks," said Sandy. "That would be really helpful."

The wedding cake was heavy and the girls picked it up carefully. Each holding a corner of the cake board, the girls slowly made their way into the barn.

WOOF! WOOF! WOOF!

Out in the field, a dog was barking at the horses. Whinnying, the horses shied away but the dog chased after them, growling and snarling nastily.

"That dog is scaring the horses," said Mia.

"Stop it! Go away!" shouted Charlotte.

Someone gave a whistle and the dog ran away from the horses.

"Phew," said Mia.

But her relief didn't last long.

The dog had left the horses alone – but now
the big white poodle was barrelling straight
towards them!

"Oh no!" Charlotte cried. "That dog is Miss
Fluffy, Hex's dog!"

"It's after the cake!" Mia shouted. They
started walking faster, but it was too late.

Barking wildly, the poodle pounced on top of
the wedding cake.

SPLAT!

The girls lost their grip on the cake and it
fell to the ground, splattering all over the dusty
path.

Miss Fluffy greedily attacked the cake,
getting crumbs stuck to her snout and icing all
over her curly fur.

"Good dog," said Hex, strolling over and patting his pet poodle. Grinning nastily, he said, "Oh dear. Was that a wedding cake? Because now it looks like a dog's dinner!"

CHAPTER FOUR

Here Comes the Bride

"Come along, Miss Fluffy," said Hex, stomping on the wedding cake as he walked off with his poodle.

"What are we going to do?" said Violet, staring at the ruined wedding cake, horrified. "There isn't time to bake another cake."

"Then we'll just have to magic up a new one," said Charlotte.

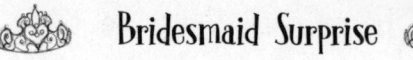

She and Mia held their glowing pendants together.

"I wish for the most delicious wedding cake!" said Charlotte.

There was a flash of light, and suddenly

the girls were holding a cupcake creation like the one Princess Sylvie had conjured up at Wishing Star Palace. There were five layers of cupcakes with swirls of sparkly silver icing. At the top there was a giant cupcake with marzipan figures of a bride and groom.

"It's incredible!" cried Violet.

They carried the cake into the barn and set it down carefully on a table.

Glancing at her watch, Violet said, "We should probably get dressed now."

As they followed Daisy and Violet to the farmhouse, Mia checked her pendant. It was glowing very faintly. "We only have one wish left," she said. "What will we do if Princess Poison comes back?"

"What we always do," said Charlotte confidently. "We'll stop her from spoiling Violet's wish. This wedding has to be perfect – Alice is counting on us."

The pretty farmhouse had a thatched roof and red roses climbing up its walls.

"Mum!" shouted Daisy, opening the door. "Where are you?"

"I'm upstairs!" her mum called back. "Come on up!"

The girls trooped upstairs and found Kate in one of the bedrooms, brushing her hair at a dressing table.

"Violet," said Kate, "you're so good at doing hair and make-up – could you do mine?"

"Of course!" said Violet, looking flattered.

"Charlotte and I can go," said Mia. "We don't want to get in the way."

"Don't be silly," said Kate. "The more the merrier!"

As Mia and Charlotte sat next to Daisy on the bed, Violet styled Kate's shoulder-length hair into a loose up-do. After fixing the bride's hair in place with a jewelled clip, Violet started

on her make-up. She gave Kate shimmering
eye shadow, rosy blush and shiny lipgloss.

"You look really pretty," said Violet.

"Thanks, sweetie," said Kate, smiling at her
soon-to-be stepdaughter.

"Mum, can I wear make-up too?" asked
Daisy. "Please ..."

"It *is* a special occasion," said Violet, winking
conspiratorially at Daisy.

"OK," said Kate. "Just a little bit."

"Yay!" said Daisy.

Violet dusted blush on Daisy's cheeks and
dabbed on some pink lipstick. "Gorgeous!" she
said, planting a kiss on the top of Daisy's head.

"I'd better put my dress on," said Kate.

Taking off her dressing gown, she slipped

into a long, cream-
coloured gown. The dress
was simple, but stunning.
It made Kate look like
a Greek goddess. The
floaty skirt skimmed
the floor, revealing just
the toes of Kate's silver
shoes.

"What do you think?"
Kate asked, twirling
around.

"Oh, Mum!" cried
Daisy, clapping her
hands. "You look
beautiful!"

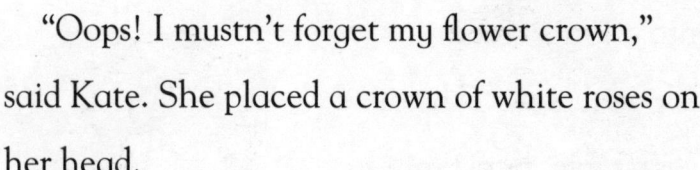

"Oops! I mustn't forget my flower crown," said Kate. She placed a crown of white roses on her head.

Violet put a few hairpins in Kate's hair to hold the crown in place. Then Daisy handed her mother a big bouquet of white lilies and roses tied with a lilac-coloured ribbon.

"That reminds me," said Kate. "I have gifts for my very helpful bridesmaids." Carefully setting down her bouquet, she handed Daisy and Violet each a small white box tied with a pretty ribbon.

"Thanks, Mum," said Daisy, eagerly opening her box. Inside was a silver necklace with a delicate pendant shaped like a flower.

"Oh!" she gasped. "It's beautiful!"

Violet opened her box and took out an identical necklace.

"Thanks, Kate," she said, putting the necklace on. Then she fastened the clasp on Daisy's necklace.

"No, thank you," said Kate. "I couldn't wish for two better bridesmaids – or two better daughters."

Daisy and Violet smiled proudly.

KNOCK! KNOCK!

"That must be the photographer," said Kate. "He wanted to take some pictures of me before the wedding. I'd better let him in."

As the bride went downstairs, Violet said to Daisy, "Let's get dressed."

The girls went over to the wardrobe and took out two lilac-coloured bridesmaid dresses. They were a similar style to Kate's wedding dress, but not as long.

Mia helped Daisy zip up her dress. "You both look really pretty," she said.

Violet smoothed down her dress. "It's not my usual style," she said. "But I like the colour." She placed a crown of light purple flowers on her head, then put one on Daisy's head too.

Daisy grinned at Violet. "We match!" she said. "We've even got the same necklaces – just like Mia and Charlotte."

"There's just one teeny tiny difference," mocked Princess Poison, magically appearing in the middle of the room. "They aren't magic. So you can't stop me from ruining the wedding."

"You're wasting your time," said Charlotte.

Ignoring Charlotte, Princess Poison strolled over to Daisy. "What a yummy dress," she said, stroking the fabric. She touched Violet's crown of flowers. "And what delicious-looking flowers." Smirking, she said, "You both look good enough to eat."

"What do you mean?" Daisy asked nervously.

Princess Poison took out her wand and uttered a spell.

"This wedding needs some hungry guests. Send caterpillars and other pests!"

The room exploded with green light. Slimy green caterpillars crawled all over the girls' flower crowns and bridesmaid bouquets.

MUNCH! CRUNCH!

The caterpillars chomped relentlessly through the flowers.

"Ugh!" said Mia, pulling a fuzzy green caterpillar off

Daisy's crown. She pulled off another – and then another. But there were just too many caterpillars. In minutes they had eaten all the petals, leaving only the stems behind.

"Oh no!" cried Violet, looking down. "My dress!"

Silvery moths had eaten the silky fabric of her dress, leaving it dotted with holes.

Charlotte tried to swat the moths away, but it was too late. The damage was done. Violet and Daisy's bridesmaid dresses were so full of holes they looked like Swiss cheese!

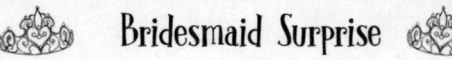

Princess Poison peered out of the window. "Your guests are starting to arrive," she said. "You might want to find something else to wear." Then, chortling to herself, she waved her wand and vanished.

CHAPTER FIVE
Wedding Crashers

Daisy and Violet ran to the window.

"Oh no," cried Violet. "Princess Poison wasn't lying. The guests are starting to arrive!" She clutched the skirt of her ruined bridesmaid dress. "What are we going to do?"

"We're going to make a wish," said Charlotte.

Mia held her pendant against Charlotte's.

Faint light glowed out of the heart. There was just enough magic left for one wish.

"I wish for the bridesmaid dresses and flowers to be even more beautiful than before," said Mia.

The wish magic gave Daisy and Violet brand new dresses. They were still made from the same silky lilac fabric, but now they were completely different styles.

Violet ran over to the mirror on the wardrobe door to check out her new dress. It had a halter neck and flared out into a short, swishy skirt. "This is exactly what I would have chosen!"

She touched her flower crown, which was bursting with sweetly scented blossoms. "And you gave me violets!"

"What else?" said Charlotte, grinning.

"Mine are daisies!" cried Daisy, joining Violet in front of the mirror. Her dress had cascading ruffles on the skirt and short, lacy sleeves.

The magic had turned the caterpillars into beautiful butterflies. They fluttered around the bedroom like colourful confetti.

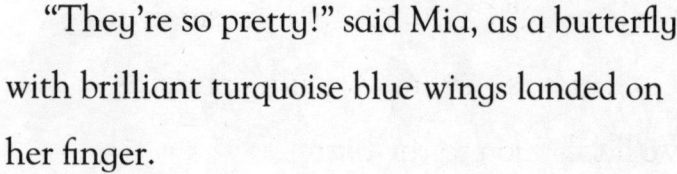

"They're so pretty!" said Mia, as a butterfly with brilliant turquoise blue wings landed on her finger.

Violet opened the window so the butterflies could fly away, but some settled on the girls' flower crowns and bouquets, making them look even more beautiful. "I guess we should go down and help show the guests in," she said.

"But I thought we were going to practise our song one more time," said Daisy anxiously.

"We can show the guests where to go," offered Charlotte.

"Yes," said Mia. "That way you can practise your song. I'm sure it's going to be great."

As Mia and Charlotte headed downstairs, they could hear Daisy and Violet rehearsing.

"Follow us," Charlotte told the smartly dressed guests carrying wedding presents. "We'll take you to the barn."

As they led the guests down the path, Mia whispered nervously, "Daisy and Violet look gorgeous, but now we don't have any wishes left! I'm so worried that Princess Poison will win this time and ruin both weddings!"

"We've stopped her without wishes before," Charlotte reminded her.

Mia and Charlotte stood at the entrance of the barn, welcoming the guests. As they filed into the barn, guests left presents on the table with the wedding cake. A folk band wearing tartan shirts played softly in the background as the guests took their seats on the hay bales.

Wearing a smart suit, Ben shook hands with guests. He made his way to the rose-covered archway, where a grey-haired lady in a navy blue dress was waiting.

"Who's that?" Charlotte said.

"I think she's the registrar," Mia said. "She does the wedding ceremony."

Once all the guests were seated, it was time for the wedding to start!

DUM DUM DEE DUM!

The band began to play the wedding march. All eyes turned to the back of the barn, waiting for the bride to make her entrance.

Daisy came down the aisle first, scattering daisy and violet petals from a basket. She was followed by Violet, who winked at the girls as she walked past. Butterflies flew off their bouquets and fluttered around the barn.

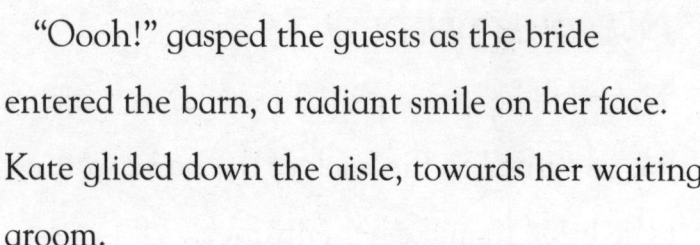

"Oooh!" gasped the guests as the bride entered the barn, a radiant smile on her face. Kate glided down the aisle, towards her waiting groom.

"She looks so happy," Mia whispered to Charlotte.

"Welcome," said the registrar, as Kate joined Ben under the archway. "We are gathered here to celebrate the wedding of two people who love each other very much. To start us off, their daughters have planned a special surprise."

The band's keyboard player let Daisy sit down at the keyboard, while Violet picked up her guitar. Playing their instruments, the girls performed the song they'd written.

"You found each other and you fell in love!"

the girls sang together. "It was written in the stars above."

By the end of the song, everyone joined in with the chorus. "You're getting married today, hooray! We wish you joy on your wedding day!"

When the song was over, the guests cheered and gave Daisy and Violet a standing ovation.

Ben and Kate clapped loudest of all, proud smiles on their faces.

"Now it is time to exchange your vows," said the registrar. Turning to Ben, she asked, "Do you, Ben, take Kate to be your lawful wedded wife?"

"I do," said Ben, gazing lovingly into his bride's eyes.

There was a commotion as two latecomers noisily entered the barn.

"Oh no," moaned Mia, as she turned and saw Princess Poison and Hex sit down behind her and Charlotte.

"And do you, Kate, take Ben to be your lawful wedded husband?" the registrar asked with a grin.

Tears of joy streamed down Kate's cheeks as she said, "I do."

"I'll give her something to really cry about," said Princess Poison. She opened up a green clutch bag and took out her wand. She aimed it at a white cushion on which two gold wedding rings were resting. Princess Poison hissed:

"Make these wedding rings go away.
That will ruin their wedding day!"

FLASH! Green light blazed out of Princess
Poison's wand and the wedding rings
disappeared!

CHAPTER SIX

Love Is All You Need

"You may now exchange rings," said the registrar, picking up the white cushion. She looked at it in surprise. "Er, where have they gone?"

"Maybe they rolled away?" said Ben.

"Can you help us look for them?" said Kate asked the guests.

Everyone scrabbled on the barn floor.

"They're looking for a needle in a haystack," said Princess Poison smugly.

Hex giggled.

"We can't let her get away with this," Mia said to Charlotte. Wringing her hands anxiously, she noticed her sapphire ring glowing. The jewel wasn't flashing, the way it did when danger was near, but instead was giving out a soft blue light.

Glancing at Charlotte's hand, Mia saw that her friend's ring was glowing, too.

174

"We can give Kate and Ben our rings," said Mia, twisting her ring off her finger. She and Charlotte had had to grant four wishes to earn their magic sapphire rings. It was hard to give up something so precious, but Mia knew it was the right thing to do. It was what any true Secret Princesses would do.

"Will they fit Kate and Ben?" Charlotte asked, slipping off her own sapphire ring.

"They're magic," said Mia with a shrug. "Let's hope so!"

"We found the rings!" cried Charlotte, running to the archway.

As Mia and Charlotte placed their sapphire rings on the white cushion, they magically transformed into plain gold wedding bands.

"Phew!" said Ben, looking relieved. "How on earth did they roll all the way to the back of the barn?"

"No idea," said Charlotte, grinning at Princess Poison who was scowling at the back of the barn.

Ben slipped a ring on to Kate's finger, then she slid the other ring on to his finger.

"I now pronounce you husband and wife!" announced the registrar. "You may kiss the bride!"

The guests clapped enthusiastically when the groom gave the bride a big kiss.

"Yay!" cheered Daisy and Violet.

As the band struck up a lively tune, the beaming bride and groom walked down the

aisle, arm in arm. Daisy and Violet followed
behind them, waving to Mia and Charlotte as
they passed.

Outside in the sunshine, waiters offered
round trays of nibbles as the wedding party
posed for photos and chatted to their guests.
The girls went over to Daisy and Violet, who
were standing with the newlyweds.

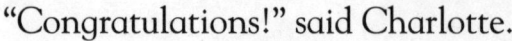

"Congratulations!" said Charlotte.

"The ceremony was beautiful," said Mia.

"We loved our song so much," said Ben.

"It was the perfect wedding present," said Kate.

"Everything about today has been perfect," said Ben, giving his new wife another kiss.

"Of course it was," said Kate. "Because we love each other. Today would have been perfect even if it had rained, or if I'd worn my oldest jeans, or if we'd had a packet of biscuits instead of a fancy wedding cake. Love is all you need for a perfect wedding."

As Violet beamed, flower petals magically rained down over the wedding party. Violet's wish had been granted!

Princess Poison glowered at Mia and Charlotte. "Ugh. Happy endings make me sick!" Yanking Hex's arm, she snarled, "Let's go!" Princess Poison jabbed her wand in the air and the wedding crashers vanished in a burst of green light.

"Good riddance!" called Charlotte.

The wedding guests moved back into the barn, sitting down at tables ready for the wedding feast. Over the band's music, Mia heard a faint voice calling her name. It was coming from her moonstone bracelet!

"Hello," she said into the white stone.

"Well done for granting Violet's wish," she heard Princess Sylvie say. "Use your ruby slippers to come back to the palace."

"We need to go back to the palace," Mia told Charlotte.

"Let's say goodbye to the girls first," said Charlotte.

They found Daisy and Violet sitting at the head table.

"We've got to go now," said Charlotte.

"But the party's just beginning," protested Daisy. "We haven't had the speeches or dancing – or the cake!"

"I wish we could stay for all the fun," said Mia. "But our princess friends need us."

"Thank you for granting my wish," said Violet. "Even though Princess Poison tried to spoil things, my dad and Kate have had a perfect wedding."

"That's because love is stronger than hate," said Mia. "Something Princess Poison will never understand."

"It was so nice sharing your special day," said Charlotte.

"And getting to know you both," added Mia.

"Thank you for helping me and Vi become friends," said Daisy.

"We're not friends any more," said Violet, laughing. "We're sisters!" She hugged Mia and Charlotte. "I hope your friend's wedding goes well, too."

"It will now that we've broken Princess Poison's curse," said Mia happily.

Waving goodbye, Mia and Charlotte slipped out of the barn. Clicking the heels of their ruby

slippers together three times, the girls said,

"Wishing Star Palace!"

The magic brought the girls to the top of the
Bell Tower. The big gold bell gleamed in the
sunshine. Mia ran her hand over the smooth,
shiny surface. "It's fixed!" she announced.

"Let's ring it to tell the Secret Princesses!"
said Charlotte.

Mia pulled the bell cord. *BING!*

Charlotte rang it a second time. *BONG!*

As the bell's deep chimes rang out over the grounds of Wishing Star Palace, the Secret Princesses arrived in the Bell Tower.

"You did it!" cried Alice, sweeping the girls up in a hug.

"Now your wedding will have good luck and happiness," said Mia.

"What would make me really happy," said Alice, "is if you and Charlotte would be my bridesmaids."

Mia and Charlotte turned to each other, their mouths dropping open in surprise.

"Are you serious?" Charlotte asked Alice.

"Of course," said Alice, her eyes sparkling.

"And I'm going to pay for your whole family to fly over from California, Charlotte."

Mia and Charlotte jumped up and down, squealing in excitement.

"We're going to be bridesmaids!" cried Mia.

"Then you'll need bridesmaid dresses," said Princess Cara. She waved her wand and

suddenly the girls were wearing gorgeous bridesmaid dresses. Mia's dress was printed with beautiful flowers, and Charlotte's had a pleated skirt dotted with sparkles.

"What do you think?" Cara asked them.

"Amazing!" Mia and Charlotte said at the same time.

"Then perfect for the two most amazing girls I know," said Alice warmly.

"I love weddings!" said Charlotte. "I can't wait for yours, Alice."

Alice laughed. "It will be here before you know it," she said. "But right now you girls need to go home."

"See you soon, Charlotte," said Mia, hugging her best friend goodbye.

"When we get to be bridesmaids!" Charlotte replied, her eyes dancing in anticipation.

Alice waved her wand and the magic sent the girls home.

Mia landed in her bedroom. Quickly gathering up her art supplies, she ran back to the kitchen to find Elsie.

"I can't believe we're going to Alice's wedding," said Elsie. "Isn't that the most exciting thing ever?"

Mia smiled. She could think of something even more exciting. Because she was going to be a bridesmaid at the wedding with her very best friend!

The End

Join Charlotte and Mia in their next Secret Princesses adventure!

Read on for a sneak peek!

Mermaid Mystery

"Yippee!" cheered Charlotte Williams as her golf ball rolled into the hole. "Hole in one!"

Charlotte and her family were playing crazy golf by the beach. Every game had a fun theme. The next one was a pirate ship!

"Race you to the pirate ship!" cried Charlotte Williams, her brown curls flying out behind her as she ran. Her twin brothers, Liam and Harvey, charged after her but Charlotte got there first.

"My turn!" said Liam. He hit a bright red golf ball with his club and it rolled down the green carpet towards the pirate ship. It stopped just short of the hole, so Liam gave it another gentle tap and it rolled in.

"I'm next!" cried Harvey. "Watch me get a hole in one!"

WHACK! He hit his blue golf ball hard. It rolled off the green carpet, hit the edge and flew into the air.

PLOP! The golf ball fell into a waterfall with a loud splash.

"Oh no!" cried Harvey, staring into the water in dismay.

"Don't worry," said Charlotte. Leaning over as far as she could, Charlotte stuck her golf club into the water and fished out Liam's golf ball. She dried it off on her top and handed it back to her little brother. "Good as new!"

"You're the best, Charlotte," said Liam, giving her a hug.

Charlotte took her turn next. "Hey, everyone," she said, hitting the ball. "What did the ocean say to the pirate?"

Mum shrugged. "No clue."

"Nothing," said Charlotte, grinning. "It just waved." She pointed at the Pacific Ocean sparkling in the California sunshine. "Get it – waved."

Mum and Dad groaned at Charlotte's joke, but Liam and Harvey laughed.

Mum jotted down their scores then they moved on to the last hole. It looked like a fairytale castle. "This reminds me of the castles back in England," said Mum.

Not long ago, Charlotte and her family had moved from England to California.

"Mmm hmm," murmured Charlotte. The crazy golf castle made her think of her best friend, Mia Thompson, who lived in England. But it wasn't because of the castles in England – it was because of a magical palace hidden in the clouds! Even though they now lived far apart, Mia and Charlotte still got to see each other at Wishing Star Palace. They got to go there because they were training to become Secret Princesses, who used magic to grant wishes!

When it was Charlotte's turn again, she

gently tapped the golf ball with her club. It rolled along the green carpet and dropped straight into the hole.

"Hole in one!" cheered Dad, giving Charlotte a high five.

Mum quickly added up the final scores. "And the winner is … Charlotte!"

"Charlotte always wins," grumbled Harvey.

"Not always," protested Charlotte.

"I can't wait until we're as big as Charlotte," said Liam.

Dad chuckled and tousled Liam's curly hair. "Be patient," he said. "I was a little brother too, but now I'm a lot taller than Auntie Liz."

As Charlotte bent down to get her golf ball out, a flash of light caught her eye. The half-heart pendant hanging from her necklace was glowing! Charlotte nearly cried out with excitement – not because she'd won, but because she was going to see Mia!

"I'll go hand in the golf things," Charlotte offered quickly, collecting her brothers' golf balls and clubs. She returned them at a little wooden hut, but instead of going straight back to her family, she ducked out of sight behind the hut.

Checking that nobody was watching, she held her glowing pendant and whispered, "I wish I could see Mia."

The radiant light from the necklace

surrounded her. Charlotte's smile was almost as bright as her pendant because she couldn't wait to see Mia! As the magic swept her away, Charlotte knew her family wouldn't be worried – no time would pass here while she was gone.

A moment later, Charlotte found herself standing in the grand entrance hall of Wishing Star Palace. She was wearing her pink princess dress and her ruby slippers. Her brown eyes widened with delight as she spotted a girl in a gold dress sitting on the bottom step of a sweeping marble staircase. There was a sparkling diamond tiara on her long, blonde hair.

"Mia!" she called happily.

Mia leapt up and ran towards Charlotte.

As they hugged each other tight, Charlotte's own diamond tiara fell off her head.

"Whoops!" said Charlotte, quickly picking it up.

"Do you suppose we'll get to start the next stage of our training today?" Mia asked Charlotte, helping her put the tiara safely back on her head.

"I really hope so!" replied Charlotte.

Hearing footsteps behind them, the girls turned around. A group of Secret Princesses were coming down the stairs in bathing suits!

"Hi, girls!" said Princess Sylvie, whose polka-dotted swimsuit was red like her hair.

She was a baker back in the real world, and she had a necklace with a pendant shaped like a cupcake.

"Are you going to the palace swimming pool?" asked Mia.

"Not today," said Princess Evie, who was wearing a floral-print bikini that matched the flower pendant on her necklace. It showed her special talent for gardening. "We're going to the Blue Lagoon."

Mia and Charlotte exchanged excited looks. They'd visited Wishing Star Palace many times, but they'd never gone to a lagoon before!

"Oooh! Can we come too?" asked Charlotte.

"Of course," said Princess Ella, who had a ruffled leopard-print swimming costume. "That's where you're going to begin the next stage of your training!"

Mia and Charlotte jumped up and down, squealing.

"Yay!" cried Mia. "We can't wait to get started!"

"Then let's use our ruby slippers," Ella suggested. "So we get there fast."

Everyone clicked the heels of their red-jewelled slippers together three times and called out, "The Blue Lagoon!"

WHOOSH!

Magic whisked them high above Wishing Star Palace and across the gorgeous grounds.

As they flew, Charlotte spotted places she and Mia had visited before – the swimming pool, the roller coaster, and the beautiful butterfly garden. Finally, she spotted a glittering aquamarine lake far below. As she got closer, Charlotte saw a waterfall cascading into the lagoon. Charlotte sat down on one of the rocks around the lagoon's edge and dipped her hand in the water. "It's so lovely!"

"Look!" cried Mia, pointing across the water. "Someone's already swimming!"

A lady with long, silvery hair waved to them from the water. Suddenly a glittering green fish tail rose up from the surface.

"Oh my gosh!" gasped Charlotte,

clutching Mia's arm.

There was a mermaid in the Blue Lagoon!

Read *Mermaid Mystery* to find out what happens next!

Bridesmaid Bouquet

Every bridesmaid needs a beautiful bouquet of flowers! Tissue paper flowers are fun and easy to make. Make lots and arrange them in a vase – or use them to have a pretend wedding. They also make great gifts. The best thing about tissue paper flowers is that they won't wilt!

What you'll need:

- Tissue paper
- Pipe cleaners
- Scissors

Instructions:

1. Lay 6-10 small sheets of tissue paper on top of each other. You can use all one colour of different colours. Starting with the shorter side, fold the bottom edge over about 2.5 cm. Flip it over and fold it on the other side. Continue flipping and folding the tissue paper. When you are done, you will have a strip of tissue paper that looks like an accordion.

2. Fold the accordion in half. Then bend the end of a pipe cleaner around it, twisting it to hold it in place, to make the flower's stem.

3. Cut rounded edges at each end of the tissue paper with your scissors.

4. Gently open up the tissue paper folds, being careful not to rip the paper. Carefully separate the layers of tissue paper to fluff up your flower petals.

5. If you make lots of flowers, you can arrange them in a vase or tie a pretty ribbon around them to make a bouquet!

Weddings Around

- Chinese brides wear a red dress and a bridesmaid holds a red umbrella over her head to bring the happy couple good luck.

- In India, the bride and bridesmaids decorate their hands with beautiful henna designs. The groom wears a ring of flowers around his neck.

- The word confetti comes from Italy. It means the sweet treats, usually sugared almonds, that wedding guests receive. Yum!

- In Germany, some newlyweds saw a log together in front of their guests, to show that they are now a team.

- Korean grooms traditionally gave their bride's mother a gift of ducks or geese, to show their loyalty. Today, they usually give carved wooden birds instead of real ones!

- Instead of cake, French weddings serve an enormous tower of cream puffs!

- In Kenya, it is the custom for a bride's father to spit on her. But he isn't being mean – he's trying to prevent her from having bad luck.

- Cheeky bridesmaids in Pakistan steal one of the groom's shoes as a joke. He has to pay them to get it back!

The World

- In the Philippines, the bride and groom release a pair of white doves into the air. Coo-ee!

- Long ago in Sweden, bridesmaids carried bouquets of stinky weeds to ward off trolls! Some still do!

- One strange Scottish tradition is for the bride and groom to be pelted with rotten food the day before the wedding. Yuck!

- In Poland, wedding guests pin money to the bride's dress, while in Portugal, guests fill the bride's shoe with money.

Secret PRINCESSES

What would you wish for?

Are you a Secret Princess?
Join the Secret Princesses Club at:

secretprincessesbooks.co.uk

Explore the magic of the
Secret Princesses and discover:

♥ Special competitions! ♥
♥ Exclusive content! ♥
♥ All the latest princess news! ♥